D0752750

First Printing, 2020
ISBN 9780578631332

The Misadventures of
Toni Macaroni
IN
The Mad Scientist

Book 1

Written by Cetonia Weston-Roy
Illustrated by Chasity Hampton

CONTENTS

My name is Antoniette Estella Jean Mae McArthur. I'm not sure I like

it, it is ~~realy~~ really long and hard to spell. Mama said that her and Dad could

not agree on who to name me after. So they just named me after all my

Grandmas. I'm not sure why I have to have a long name because they

could not ~~decid~~ decide. I told Mama so, but she gave me her tiger lady look, so

I just think it to myself now. Besides ANYTHING is better than what

my Dad calls me! Because of him everyone calls me Toni Macaroni! He says

its because my arms and legs are skinny like ~~nooduls~~ noodles. Even kids in my

class call me that now, I cant live it down! I ~~thretened to sew~~ threatened to sue, but that

just made them ~~laff~~ laugh more. Being seven is not all I thought it would be. Its

not my ~~falt~~ fault my arms and legs are so skinny, Daddy says they are skinny

because I am too picky. I know that is not ~~rite~~ right because I eat all of Mommys

cooking. He just cooks like a mad ~~sientist~~ scientist! Just the other ~~nite~~ night he tried

to feed us worms for dinner! Mama swears it was just really overcooked

~~nooduls~~ noodles, but I have NEVER seen overcooked ~~nooduls~~ noodles wiggle. I told her

so but she just said I was being ~~dramatic~~ dramatic, whatever that means. Anyway,

thats pretty much how I ended up on a hunger strike. Its been two days since I started my hunger strike. So far so good, Mommy cooked both those

days I think I am wearing him down! Hunger strikes are easy!

Chapter 1: Breakfast Bust

It was a lazy Saturday morning when IT happened! I knew as soon as my eyes opened that Daddy was cooking when the smoke alarm went off downstairs. I was going to shut my eyes and wait for mommy to remake breakfast. Then I remembered what Mommy said when she tucked me in last night. She was going on a... Girls Weekend! How could she!? She knew I was on a hunger strike!

I jumped out of bed then sank to the floor. I was just about to freak out when I locked eyes with Sir-Hops-A-Lot. I took a deep breath, stood at attention and saluted.

"Sorry sir, I almost lost it there! What should I do?" I asked him. Sir-Hops-A-Lot hopped out of his tank and onto the floor.

"Pull yourself together soldier, get down there and check out the damage!" He croaked. He was right, as always. I ran to my closet and suited up in my black ninja suit from last Halloween.

I put on my glasses then grabbed walkie-talkies, my jump rope, binoculars, and a mirror. I tied the rope around my waist and stuck my gear in it. I was ready for this dangerous mission. I left one walkie-talkie next to Sir Hops-A-Lot and creaked opened my door.

The first challenge was getting past the twins' room. Zora was always awake in her crib and sounded like a screech owl anytime she saw someone walk past.

I rolled across the hall and put my back against the wall. I slowly held my mirror out to the opening to see if she was looking my way. The coast was clear. I was just about to go, when suddenly a noise came from my walkie talkie. I saw Zora whip around toward me.

I hid and fumbled to press the button, "What do you want Sir-Hops-A-Lot? You almost blew my cover," I hissed into the walkie.

A throaty "RIBBIT" was all the explanation I got.

I turned off my walkie and peeked in my mirror again. When she finally turned around, I leapt past the door. I meant to roll and land on all fours; instead, I landed on my face.

As if that wasn't embarrassing enough, I looked
up to see J, my big brother, shake his head at me as
he went up to his room. I shook the stars out of my
eyes, straightened my glasses, and crept to the stairs
to peek down into the kitchen.

Smoke was pouring from the kitchen, and
smells worse than Zora and Zaire's diaper garbage
smacked me in the nose. The smoke seemed to gath-
er into a skull and crossbones, warning me of what
was ahead.

I gathered all my courage and crawled down the stairs. When I got to the landing, I hid behind the house plant and grabbed my binoculars to peer inside the kitchen. I could see the monstrosity on the table. Was he really about to serve this to us?! It was sitting in the skillet my Granny passed down to my mom. I'd only seen yummy food come from that skillet, so seeing that mess almost brought tears to my eyes.

I looked around the kitchen, hoping to see my Dad getting ready to throw it out. I was just about to move closer for a better look when a voice sounded from behind me.

"Good morning Toni Macaroni, I didn't know you were up. Go get washed up and dressed for breakfast. I'm going to finish up some work and then we'll eat. I made something special for us!" said my Dad.

I grabbed my walkie and ran back up the stairs shouting into it, "ABORT MISSION, RETREAT!" This morning and mission were complete fails!

Chapter 2: The Mad Scientist

After getting washed and dressed I threw myself on my bed. "I can't believe I didn't check if he was in his room first!" My parents' room is right off of the stair landing, what a rookie mistake! I grabbed Sir-Hops-A-Lot and laid him on my bed. "Why didn't you tell me he wasn't in the kitchen?" I pouted.

He adjusted his little red hat and croaked back, "It's not my fault you turned off the walkie, I tried to warn you!" I stuck my tongue out at him since I couldn't say anything else to that.

"Well anyway, I have bigger problems. Now he expects me to eat it!" I exclaimed. "You can't avoid it, just go down and eat it. It can't be that bad," he answered. I rolled my eyes and put him in his tank. I was not about to take advice about food from a guy who munches on bugs.

When I got downstairs J had already left for his friend's house and the twins were in their highchairs. Lucky for them, they didn't eat big people food yet. I had never been more jealous of the twins' mushed food.

What I saw through the binoculars did not look any better up close. The skillet contained lopsided blobs that I was sure were supposed to be biscuits.

I had never seen biscuits that looked blacker than the skillet they were spilling from though.

"Daddy, how'd you get the biscuits so black and burnt?" I asked.

"Baby that's just a little color, you can scrape off the top," he answered from the stove. Somehow, I highly doubted scraping them would make it any better. They looked like they were burnt all the way through!

"Besides," he continued, "this gravy I made will go on the top and make it softer. I spiced up your Granny's recipe." He said this proudly as he sat down a bowl of what was clearly toxic sludge in front of me.

Whenever Granny really "threw down" on Thanksgiving, Mama always said she "put her foot in it." I know that's just a saying, but the stuff in front of me looked like my Daddy walked outside, then ACTUALLY put his foot in it.

"Um, Daddy, what's all that floating in it?" I asked trying to keep calm.

"We didn't have any sausage left for the gravy, so I used some canned meat I found in the back of the cabinet. You didn't know ya' daddy was an innovator did you?" He threw back his head and did that hearty laugh of his. He looked every bit of the mad scientist he is.

I could NOT eat these dirt clod biscuits with toe jam gravy. I had to think of a way out of this and FAST. I did the only thing I could think of. I teetered side to side in my chair, then fell onto the kitchen floor with a huge BUMP. I'd seen the ladies in the old movies Granny watches do that countless times. I made sure to keep my eyes shut tight. Then I placed the back of my hand on my forehead so that my faint was more convincing.

I was glad Mommy wasn't home now. When I tried this with her, she left me on the floor until I gave up and got up. Right on cue, I heard my dad jump up and call my name. I didn't answer until he came over and picked me up.

I opened my eyes slightly and softly said, "Daddy, I'm not feeling so good. Can I lay back down?" I saw his eyes flood with relief, I had him!

"Sure Baby Girl, I'll take you to the couch." He got me some water and laid me on the couch. "Do you need anything else Honey?" he asked. Before I could answer his phone rang.

"Hey, Ma! No, she left for her Girls' trip already. It's just me and the kids," he spoke into the phone. "I'm not sure you should still come by, Toni may be sick." My eyes popped open as I realized he was talking to Granny Odie. Luckily, my Granny still wanted to see her Granddaughter; and Daddy almost never said no to her.

Daddy packed the twins' bag for their appointments and got ready to go. It was a miracle! This was a way out of Dad's awful home-cooked meals, and I had almost the whole day to come up with a plan of attack.

Chapter 3: The Granny Gauntlet

When Granny got to our house she told me to keep resting on the couch and she turned on some cartoons. This weekend was looking up already! As I laid there content, a wonderful smell started to drift from the kitchen. I skipped to the kitchen and climbed up onto a chair.

"Whatcha cookin'?" I asked. She didn't answer, but she brought out the skillet with her homemade biscuits. They were the complete opposite of what Dad made. They were made right! My mouth watered as I watched her mix a pot on the stove. It could only be her world-famous sausage gravy.

"Grab a bowl, Honey." she grinned. I ran to the cupboard, got a bowl and held it out expectantly. Instead of delicious biscuits and gravy, she plopped gray, lumpy oatmeal in my bowl. I looked up at her feeling betrayed. She just looked at me with that little smile that's always on her face.

"Your Daddy told me you fainted at the breakfast table and that you're feeling sick." I saw a gleam in her eye as she continued, "Plain oatmeal is all sick people should eat."

I was caught, I either had to come clean or eat the oatmeal. I could tell that this was a test of my strength. So I just nodded and sat down in front of my bowl of oatmeal. I took a spoonful and grasped a single grain between my teeth to chew.

YUCK! I normally don't like oatmeal but I really didn't like this goop that had no butter or sugar to disguise the grossness.

I looked over at my granny hoping to gain some sympathy. There was no sympathy, only the same amused smile. I knew I couldn't lose this battle! I shoveled the oatmeal in as fast as I could. I took sips of orange juice in between bites to mask the taste.

Finally, my bowl was clean. I sat up triumphantly and looked at my granny with a smile of my own. It quickly slid off my face when I saw her smile was even bigger...uh oh.

"I'm so glad you have your appetite back, I'll get you more!" she chirped happily.

"NO, MA'AM! Uhhh, I mean I'm not feeling so good. Can I lay down again?" I asked. As soon as the words left my mouth I knew I should've left it at no.

"Well that just won't do, I'll fix you up!" as she said this, she slung me under her arm with surprising strength.

She carried me to the living room and sat me gently on the edge of the couch. She pulled out vapor rub from her big purse and began slathering it on the bottom of my feet, my chest and my nose. Then she pulled out her quilt and wrapped me tightly in it. Now I know how a burrito feels!

She turned on the channel with the old movies that they forgot to put color in and told me she'd be back. I was hot from being wrapped up and had that gross vapor rub all over me. On top of it all, this movie stunk!

After what seemed like forever, she came back in and shuffled over to the couch to feel my forehead.

"Oh my, you're feeling very warm. I'd better get my oil."

My Granny had a special bottle of oil that she put on our foreheads when we were sick or "acting up." She always put too much and it ended up dripping down our face- which is exactly what happened in this case.

The biggest problem was that I didn't have my hands free to wipe it off when she wasn't looking like usual. As the oil trickled slimily down my head, I had had enough!

"Granny, I have to use the bathroom, my tummy doesn't feel so good. Can you get me out of this!?" She looked at me for a long moment then let me out; I ran to the bathroom. As soon as I shut the door, I grabbed a towel and wiped off the oil and the vapor rub.

I tiptoed out of the bathroom to find a place to hide for a while, but Granny was waiting.

"How is your stomach feeling Toni?" she asked. She had something behind her back; was she going to make me eat more oatmeal if I said I was fine?!

"It still hurts a little bit," I said softly, not meeting her eyes.

"Well, in that case, some castor oil will clean you right out!" She said as she pulled a glass bottle and a spoon from behind her back.

"Open wide!" She smiled as she poured the thick, oily goop into the spoon. That was it! I couldn't do it anymore!

"Granny no, I'm so sorry for telling stories! I'm not sick and I never was!"

The words poured out faster, "Please don't make me eat that, I really am fine. I just didn't want to eat Daddy's cooking!" She looked at me with a smile then poured the castor oil carefully back into the bottle.

"So that's what was going on. I accept your apology. Still, it's not good to tell lies, no matter the reason Sugar." she said softly.

I nodded my head and looked down feeling ashamed. "Let's talk about it over some food," she said, as she hugged me and led me back to the kitchen.

I had survived Granny's challenges! I didn't "win" but somehow I felt much better this way!

I sat with Granny in the kitchen while talking through bites of her wonderful cooking. I told her about Daddy's awful cooking and how I was on a hunger strike. She laughed that deep laugh where her round little belly seemed to laugh with her.

"Does he know you're on a hunger strike?" she asked between chuckles.

"Well, no... And Mommy cooked all the other days of my hunger strike."

"Does he even know that you don't like the way he cooks?" she asked.

I thought about it.

"I guess I never really said anything. Mommy usually does it." I said.

"Sugar, it's always best to be honest, open, and straightforward with your beliefs and your actions," she said calmly. "You should tell him how you feel and find a way to work with him." Granny always knows the best things to say. She was right, all I have to do is tell Daddy how I feel and it'll all work out!

Granny glanced at the clock. "Your Daddy should be home soon with your brother and sister, are you ready to talk to him?" she asked. I jumped down from my chair and nodded my head. She chuckled, "You go, Girl!" With Granny's advice, I could do no wrong!

Chapter 4: Truth Trials

When Daddy got back, I waited for him to put the twins down for a nap. I gave him a big hug to welcome him home and thanked Granny for spending time with me.

As Granny left, she winked at me as if to say, 'Remember what I said.' I smiled at her so she would know I had this in the bag!

I turned to face Daddy with my mind made up.

"You still feeling sick Toni Macaroni?" he asked.

I took a deep breath and confessed. "Daddy, I'm sorry I lied earlier. I wasn't really feeling sick." I hung my head as he looked down at me in surprise.

"That's not like you," he said as he sat down and pulled me onto his lap. "Why would you lie to me about being sick?" he asked.

It was the moment of truth; my Granny's advice about being honest and straightforward rang in my head as I looked him straight in the eyes.

"Daddy, that breakfast you made looked terrible." His face went from curious to dumbfounded.

I looked down and continued, "I don't like any of your cooking! It always looks gross whenever you cook, like a bad science experiment! And it doesn't just look bad, it tastes triple bad! I know you don't cook a lot, but maybe you should leave it to Mommy. I think we should just get some pizza until she gets back!"

I let out a breath as I ended and looked up expecting to see understanding. Instead, I saw anger and something I didn't recognize. It made my tummy squeeze up in a knot.

Luckily, I didn't have to find out what it was because Zaire screeched awake from his nap. Daddy took me off his lap and went upstairs to grab them. He stopped halfway and looked back at me. "You can eat what I make or you can go to bed hungry," he said firmly and stomped up the stairs.

I couldn't believe it! Granny was wrong, it wasn't better to be straightforward. Daddy was mad at me for the first time in my wholeee life!

My eyes stung as I ran up the stairs and into my room. I shut my door and flopped onto my beanie chair. I looked up at Sir-Hops-A-lot's tank to find him looking down at me expectantly.

"What did you do now?" he croaked with an eye roll.

I sat up and looked at him, hurt. "Whose side are you on?! I didn't do a single thing! Daddy is being unreasonable!" I pouted. "Why do I have to be hungry because he cooks bad food?!"

Sir-Hops-A-Lot jumped from his tank and down onto my chest. "Did you say that?" He asked.

"Yessss, I told him straightforward just like Granny said and he got mad!" I said exasperatedly.

"Well, she told you to be straightforward, not straight rude. Your dad doesn't cook a lot. Have you ever watched to see why he cooks like that?" He reasoned. I thought about it, " You're right!!" I exclaimed.

"As usual," stated Sir-Hops-A-Lot. "You have to observe the enemy in order to defeat them, good thinking!" I said. I had to fight fire with fire. I had to prepare for battle! I can't give up just like that! What would Granny say?! The hunger strike is just beginning!

Chapter 5: The Hungry Strike

I woke up to my tummy rumbling the next day. Daddy didn't budge and sent me to bed when I wouldn't eat dinner. He didn't come to get me for breakfast either! Which was okay because now I had time to strategize.

Mommy was going to be back around lunchtime today. Daddy would probably start cooking lunch soon to celebrate Mom coming home. If I could just hold on until dinner, Mommy will probably cook. But I'm starving so much now! If I can put up a bigger fuss maybe I can get him to order out for lunch.

I turned to Sir-Hops-A-Lot, "Are you ready to go on strike!"

"You're buggin', don't get me involved!" he groaned. I rolled my eyes scooped him up and put him in my front pocket anyway. Lucky for us, my other Grandma did a lot of protesting and she told me plenty of stories about how to get it done!

I decided to start with a sit-in. I went downstairs with my step stool in tow. I saw Daddy on the couch watching football. I walked in silently, put my step stool in front of the TV, and plopped down.

"Toni, I can't see! Move out of the way!" I stayed silent and firmly in my seat, hoping he got the message loud and clear. I shall not be moved! He picked me up, chair and all, and moved me out of the way.

Okayyy, so maybe I can be moved, but I could wear him down by not giving up! We went back and forth like this until he got tired of it.

He picked me up, laid me on the couch and squished me with his legs until I promised not to go back in front of the TV.

Since the subtle approach didn't work, I decided to go strong with another idea from Grandma. She said sometimes people wrote their feelings on buildings with graffiti to protest unfair situations. So I grabbed some crayons and the twins, and we went to work on the living room wall in the name of justice!

That really didn't end well. All I got was a bunch of scrubbing, sore fingers, and some time in the shame corner. Daddies really don't appreciate civil unrest, I wouldn't recommend it.

"UGHHH, back to the drawing board!" I complained to Sir-Hops-A-Lot as I retreated to my room.

"I told you this wasn't a good idea, but you're hard-headed!" He said, from the bottom of my pocket.

I mustered all the thinking power I had left. I could hear pots and pans beginning to bang downstairs. Finally, an idea popped into my head.

I grabbed some poster board, markers, and tape from Mommy's craft room. I dragged it all to my room and plopped it onto the floor.

"What are you planning to do with all of that?" asked Sir-Hops-A-Lot.

"Everyone knows that every strike needs signs to work!" I replied. I can't believe I didn't think of it sooner!

I sat down and studied my supplies, what could I write to get my point across? I grabbed my red marker and carefully wrote

"No Justis, No Peece!"

I stepped back to admire my handy work. I'm one of the best spellers in my class, but something didn't look quite right. I started to call out for my Dad but stopped myself. I couldn't consult the enemy on spelling!

I drew a peace sign and a few glittery hearts. After all, even protest signs should be cute! I taped a bunch of paper towel rolls together and taped them to my sign for a handle. I was ready to fight!

Chapter 6: Revolution Resolution

As I headed down the stairs with my sign in hand, it looked like a bomb went off downstairs. The twins were screaming, and one was running around with their diaper off. J was tearing up the house looking for his basketball shoes while scarfing down a sandwich and getting dressed. Dad was trying to help him as he held Zora under his arm and attempted to capture bare-bottomed Zaire.

I could smell something burning in the kitchen. Daddy seemed to notice at the same time because he shouted then placed Zora on the ground and ran towards the kitchen.

"J put Zaire's diaper back on for me!" He said. He glanced at me and my sign and muttered under his breath as he went into the kitchen. I decided it was too loud for me to chant, so I just sat there watching the chaos with my sign.

Zora's diaper was only part of the way on when she decided she wanted to be like Zaire. It was fun seeing both of them without a diaper until Zaire decided to treat J like a diaper!

"DAAAD, ZAZA JUST PEED ON ME!" yelled
a horrified J. Dad came running back in with oven
mitts on.

"Quick! Go shower and change your clothes, the
Johnson's will be here to pick you up for practice any
second!" He tried to catch the twins as they made
their escape. As I watched the chaos, I realized what
Sir-Hops-A-Lot and Granny meant.

When Mommy cooks, Daddy is there to take care of us. But Daddy only cooks when Mommy is gone, and no one was here to help him. Sir-Hops-A Lot seemed to realize what I was thinking because he popped out of my pocket and looked at me expectantly. I pushed him back in; I already felt bad enough. Daddy was trying his best and I just said mean things to him.

I put down my sign and went to catch Zora. I grabbed her and looked at Daddy.

"I'll put diapers on the twins, you can finish cooking." He looked at me with surprise and then smiled.

"Thanks, Toni Macaroni."

As he went back into the kitchen I rounded up the twins by showing them Sir-Hops-a-lot and then put on their diapers one at a time like Mama showed me. I crawled on the ground with them and kept them busy until Daddy came back.

"Do you need help setting the table?" I asked.

"No, I was just letting you know dinner is already burnt to a crisp. What kind of pizza do you want?" He said, with a tired grin. I smiled and gave him a hug.

"Thank you Daddy, and I'm sorry. I should have told you how I felt without being rude and asked if I could help! Let's clean up before Mama gets home!" He smiled and picked me up into a big hug.

I guess the hunger strike didn't work out for me, but everything feels like it ended up the best way it could!

"Apology accepted Toni..." Daddy said, interrupting my thoughts, "...but you aren't getting off that easy! Am I telling your mom you drew on the walls or are you?"

THE END

A big thanks to my family and friends who spent countless hours helping me on this journey! Thank you to the over-imaginative little girl that still lingers in my heart and yelled to be let out!